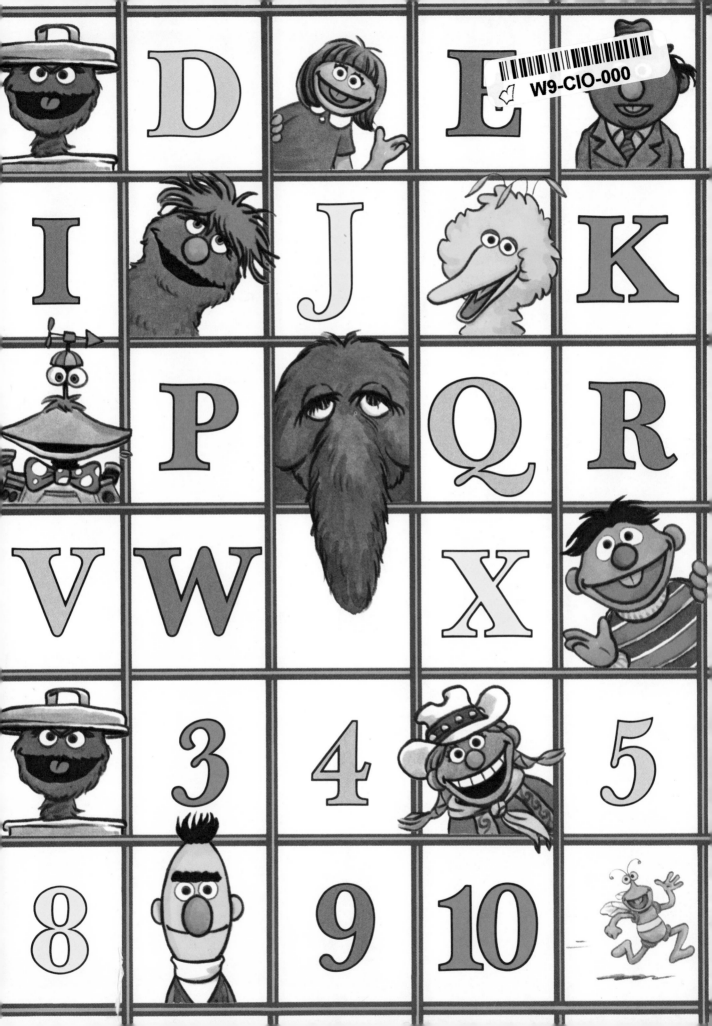

THE SESAME STREET
TREASURY

Featuring Jim Henson's Sesame Street Muppets

VOLUME 15

STARRING
THE NUMBER
15
AND THE LETTERS
X, Y, AND Z

Children's Television Workshop/Funk & Wagnalls, Inc.

WRITTEN BY:

Linda Bove with the
National Theatre of the Deaf
Michael Frith
Jocelyn Gunnar
Emily Perl Kingsley
Sharon Lerner
Jeffrey Moss
Norman Stiles
Pat Thackray
Ellen Weiss
Daniel Wilcox

ILLUSTRATED BY:

Tom Cooke
Mel Crawford
A. Delaney
Larry DiFiori
Mary Grace Eubank
Michael Frith
Randy Jones
Joe Mathieu
Marc Nadel
Maggie Swanson

PHOTOGRAPHS BY:

Charles Rowan
Neil Selkirk
View-Master International Group

Name That Fifteen!

"Hello, hello, hello, everyone. This is Guy Smiley, your host on the TV game show everybody loves—*Name That Fifteen!* And our special guest today is that lovable, furry blue monster, Grover! Let's hear it for Grover!"

"Yaaay!" yelled everyone in the studio audience.

"Now, Grover, tell us a little bit about yourself. What do you do?"

"Well, Mr. Smiley, I really like to—"

"That's very nice, Grover. And now for our first question: How many toes does a fifteen-toed boola-bird have?"

Grover thought and thought. Finally he was ready to answer.

"Fifteen?" he guessed.

A bell rang and Guy Smiley clapped his hands. "Yes! Fifteen!" he yelled. "What a smart monster.

"Now," said Guy Smiley. "Here comes a tougher question: For how many minutes should you boil a fifteen-minute egg?"

Grover scratched his head. He did a little counting on his fingers. Then he answered.

"Fifteen," said Grover. "Fifteen minutes."

This time bells and buzzers sounded. "You're right again! Fifteen minutes!" shouted Guy Smiley. "This is incredible! But let's see how you do with a really tough one: A man needs fifteen elephants. Should he buy a five-elephant package, a nine-elephant package, or a fifteen-elephant package?"

Grover was catching on now. "This is not hard," he said. "He should definitely buy the fifteen-elephant package. I bet it is cheaper that way too."

"Ha, ha, ha!" Guy Smiley laughed as the bells and buzzers went off and lights flashed. "What a mind! What a funny-bone!

"Now, Grover," said Guy Smiley in a whisper, "I want you to think carefully. Do you want to go on to the really big one—the jackpot question?"

A hush fell over the crowd.

"Yes," said Grover. "This is so easy it is ridiculous."

"Well, just wait until you hear this one: How many rings does a fifteen-ring circus have?"

"Fifteen!" said Grover. "This is really boring."

The crowd went wild.

"Grover!" shouted Guy Smiley. "You have done an amazing thing! You've won every prize that we have! Let's see what you've won!"

"Oh, I am so happy!" said Grover. "Will it be a trip around the world? A new toaster? Or may I just take the money?"

"No, it's better than that!" said Guy Smiley. "Just look at these prizes! A fifteen-toed boola-bird!"

"What?" said Grover.

"A fifteen-minute egg!"

"Oh, wait a minute," said Grover.

"Look at this! Fifteen elephants!" screamed Smiley. "Oops, better get out of the way."

Grover was hiding his eyes. "I would just like a toaster, please," he said.

"And will you look at this? An entire fifteen-ring circus!" cried Guy Smiley. "Now, Grover, I have just one more question: When would you like your prizes delivered?"

Grover thought for a minute and then replied, "How about in fifteen years?"

The Great Sesame Street Alphabet Show

ABCD...
First—the Incredible
Alphabet Acrobats!

EFGH...
Next—the Great Bert
and his sensational flying PIGEONS!

IJKLM...
Here is the fantastic
Balancing Bird—oops!

NOPQ...
And now—The Amazing Mumford's
Magic Letters—
A la peanut butter sandwiches!

RSTUV...
Presenting Oscar and his Wonder-worms,
starring SLIMEY as the letter S!

WXYZ...
And last of all... The Mighty Monsters!
What a show!

The Two-Headed Monster

Home:	1 plus 1 Sesame Street
Favorite Food:	Grape Popsicles with two sticks
Favorite Drink:	Ice-cream sodas with two straws
Best Friends:	The Honkers
Favorite Activity:	Helping children cross the street safely after school
Pet Peeve:	Double-talk
Favorite Song:	"I've Got Two"
Favorite Wish:	To sing in two-part harmony

I have this poem here about body parts.
My friends are going to show you what they are.

Ankle, Shoulder, Knee
by Big Bird

Oh! A knee is kinda roundish, like an orange or an egg;
You'll find it sticking out, right in the middle of your leg.
It bends right in the middle when you want to run or jump;
It's a funny kinda, lumpy kinda, knobby kinda bump.

> Oh! A.B C D – 1, 2, 3,
> Let's all sing a song about a knee!

Oh! A shoulder is the joint that's at the top part of your arm,
And everybody's got 'em, in the city or the farm.
It's so useful when you want to wave hello or wave good-bye,
And wiggling it up and down is easy if you try.

> Oh! A B C – When you are older,
> Hope you'll remember this song about a shoulder.

Oh! An ankle can be found at the beginning of your foot,
And when you're getting dressed, it's in the sock that it is put.
An ankle is important if you want to dance or run,
And if anybody kicks you there, it isn't any fun.

> Oh! A B C – A jinkle and a jankle,
> It's hard to find a rhyme
> For a silly word like ankle.

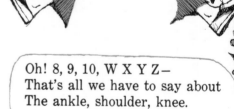

> Oh! 8, 9, 10, W X Y Z –
> That's all we have to say about
> The ankle, shoulder, knee.
>   Wheeee!

When you think about your body
And you think of all its parts,
Don't only think of eyes and ears,
Of noses, mouths, and hearts...
Think of the parts that move and bend,
That help both you and me
To walk and run and jump and play–
The ankle, shoulder, knee.

Ernie Buys a Z

As Ernie walked down the street one day, he heard a "Pssst!" from nearby. He looked around and saw a shifty-looking Salesman hiding behind a tree.

"C'mere, kid," said the Salesman. "I'm gonna show you something that'll save you pain and trouble." And out from under his coat he took a big letter **Z**.

"That's the letter **Z**," said Ernie. "How will it save me pain and trouble?"

"I'll explain," said the Salesman. "Suppose you're at a party. And suppose somebody at the party asks you what the first letter is in the word **zebra**. And you can't remember."

"Oh, dear," said Ernie. He was imagining the party. He could just see it. Everybody would be pointing at him, and saying he couldn't spell. They'd probably never invite him to another party. If only he could remember the first letter in **zebra**!

"But," said the Salesman, "if you had this **Z**, you could take it out, look at it, and it would remind you that the first letter in **zebra** is **Z**."

"Thank goodness for that **Z**," said Ernie. "It's great for parties."

"Right," said the Salesman. "And there's another way it can help you. Suppose you're on a quiz show. The prize is two million dollars, *plus* a trip around the world, *and* a carton full of rubber duckies . . ."

"Wowee!" said Ernie. "What a prize!"

The Salesman went on, "Your question is: What's the first letter in the word **zoo**? But you can't remember. The seconds are ticking by . . .

. . . the band is playing tense music. . . ."

Ernie could just picture the whole thing. There he was, on the quiz show. If he couldn't answer the question, he'd get no prize! Everybody would boo him! If only he could remember the first letter in **zoo**!

"Well," said the Salesman, "if you had this **Z**, it would remind you that the first letter in **zoo** is **Z**."

"That settles it!" said Ernie. "I've got to have that **Z**! It'll save me pain and trouble!"

So Ernie bought the **Z** and walked away with it down the street.

The Salesman was about to leave when a stranger came up, holding a microphone. "HI!" he said. "I'm GUY SMILEY, and *you* are on QUIZ SHOW IN THE STREET! Today's prize is TWO MILLION DOLLARS, *PLUS* A TRIP AROUND THE WORLD, *AND* A CARTON FULL OF RAINCOATS! And TODAY'S QUESTION is: WHAT IS THE FIRST LETTER IN THE WORD **ZERO**?"

And to Guy Smiley's surprise, the Salesman ran away down the street shouting, "Hey, kid! Come back here with that letter!"

There! Now this the **Y** page!
Now everything belong!
And you know something?
This letter *delicious!!*

GENTE EN MI VECINDARIO

PEOPLE IN MY NEIGHBORHOOD

Say it in Spanish!

médico
doctor

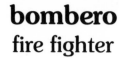

bombero
fire fighter

cartero
mail carrier

fotógrafo
photographer

bibliotecario
librarian

trabajadores de construcción
construction workers

barbero
barber

almacenero
grocer

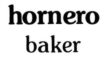

hornero
baker

The Count's Counting Page

Oh, look at all the steps!
I'm climbing all the steps!
I'm counting all the wonderful steps!
Oh, look at all the steps!
I think that I'll play in my attic today . . .
And then I can count all the steps on the way!

How many steps are there?

Larry Di Fiori

Bert had a bright new shiny red yo-yo. "If I really practice," he said to himself, "I will be able to amaze and astound my friends with the tricks I can do."

So Bert practiced. He tried "Rock the Cradle." He tried "Walking the Dog." He tried "Slurp the Soup" and "Skip to My Lou" and "Wash the Floor." But the more he practiced, the more tangled the string became. Soon there was no more string wrapped around the yo-yo. It was all wrapped around Bert!

"Well." Bert sighed. "I guess I'll have to amaze and astound everyone with my paper clip collection instead!"

Say it in sign language! **The Alphabet**

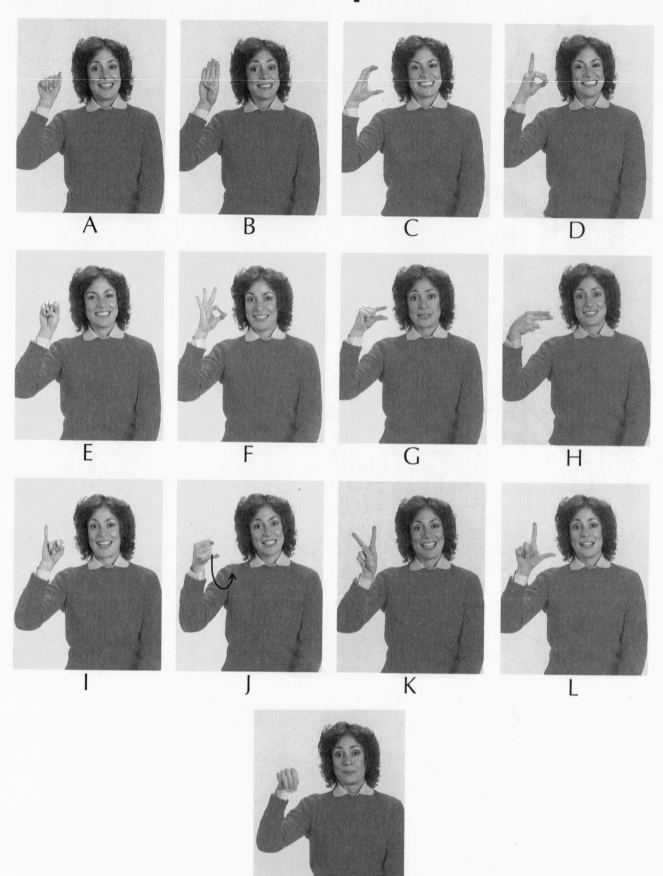

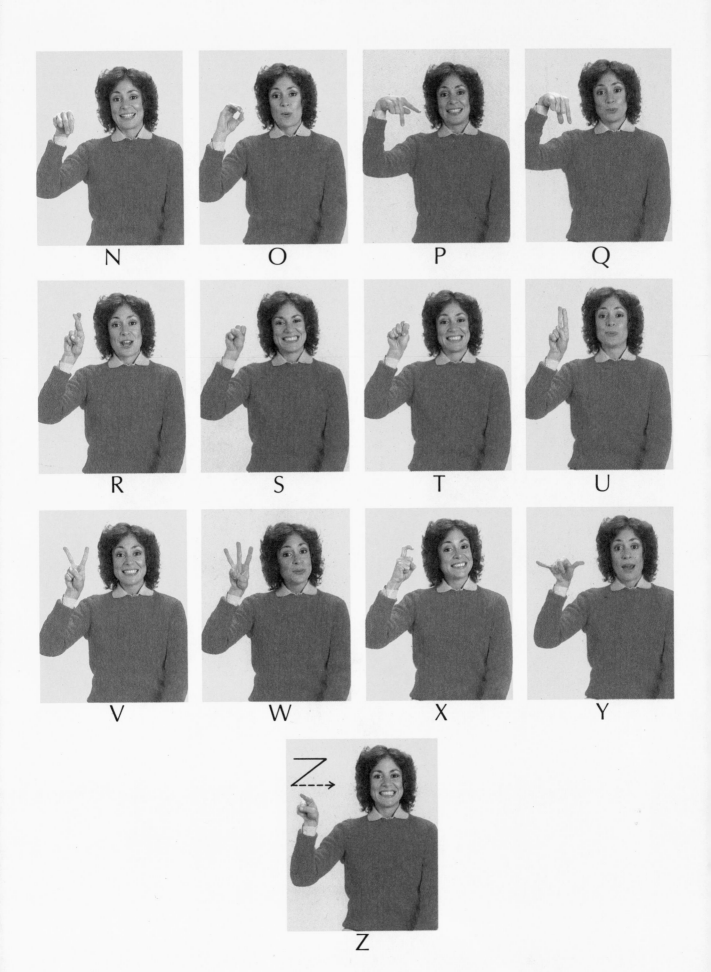

Numbers

3

4

1

2

5

6

7

8

9

10

Cookie Monster's Alphabet Cookies

First, you need to make cookie dough! If you look in Volume 1 it will tell you all about how to do that. O.K., cookie dough ready? Here we go!

Oh! Me, Cookie, finally remember to give you recipe for Alphabet Cookies.

1. Have a grownup heat oven to 400 degrees.

2. Put cloth on table. Sprinkle with **flour**.

3. Roll out dough on cloth, about ¼ inch thick.

4. Cut dough into strips.

5. Use strips of dough to make your FAVORITE letters.

ABCDEFGHIJKLMNOPQRSTUVWXYZ

6. Put cookie letters on ungreased cookie sheet.

7. O.K. Now comes HARDEST part of all . . . Put in oven (have a grownup help!) and WAIT six to eight minutes. OH . . . ME hate this waiting around . . . Me have little snack while me wait . . .

TABLE! (Yum, yum!)
CHAIR! (Munch, crunch)

POTS! PANS! ROLLING PIN! (Oh, boy! Gobble)
EGGBEATER! SINK!
(Oof, Umf)

Hey, me think cookies about ready now . . . just in time for dessert.

Boy, that sure was a good sink . . .

Grover and the
Twenty-Six Scoops

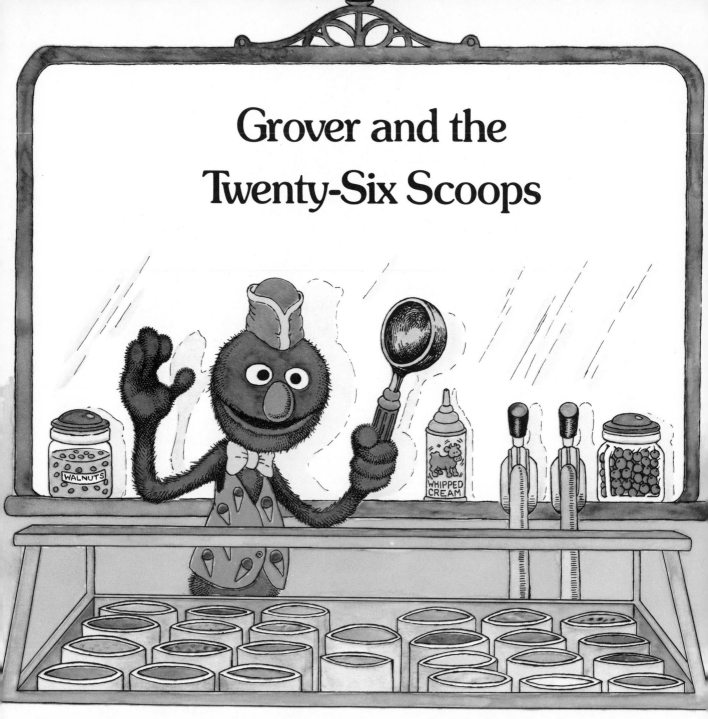

It was Grover's first day as an ice-cream scooper at Ye Olde ABC Ice-Cream Parlor. He stood proudly behind the counter, his brightly polished scoop in hand, ready to help his first customers. In came Betty Lou and her little brother, Herbie.

"Greetings, little girl and little boy," said Grover, peering up over the counter. "Welcome to Ye Olde

ABC Ice-Cream Parlor. The Special of the Week is . . ."

"Please, sir," said Betty Lou. "I already know what I want—a double-dip Vanilla cone, no sprinkles. What do you want?" she asked Herbie.

"Well . . . ummmm . . . errrr . . . geeee . . . I don't know," said Herbie. "What flavors do you have?"

"We have twenty-six terrific

flavors," said Grover. "One for each letter of the alphabet, and I know them all by heart. At Scoop School we had to recite them every morning after breakfast."

"Twenty-six flavors!" said Herbie. "Oh, boy, I want to hear them all."

"Oh, no," groaned Betty Lou. "Herbie, you know you can never make up your mind."

"I want to hear every flavor," said Herbie.

"Certainly," said Grover. "You are the customer, and the customer is always right. Are you ready? Here we go!"

"Wait, mister," said Herbie. "I can't see into the ice-cream bins."

"You are right, little boy," said Grover. "I will show you each delicious flavor."

Grover whipped out a cone and scooped out the first flavor as he proudly called its name. "Starting with the letter A we have Anchovy Applesauce.... Next, B—Baloney Bonbon, C—Cactus Crunch, D—Dinosaur Dip, E—Eggplant Eclair, F—Fruitcake Fiesta Flip," sang Grover, scooping one brightly colored flavor on top of another. "G—Gumball Goop, H—Honey Hamburger Hash, I—for Imitation Igloo ..." Grover stopped a minute to catch his breath.

"What's next?" asked Herbie excitedly.

"Next?" said Grover. "Next we have this sweet little flavor that begins with J—Jiffy Jellybean Jive. And then we have K for Kangaroo Kringle, and here's the bin for L—L for Lavender Licorice."

"Can you wait a minute, mister?" asked Herbie. "I can't keep up with all the flavors."

"I am sorry, little Herbie," said Grover. "I cannot stop or I will lose my place in the alphabet. Then I will have to start all over again from the beginning."

"From the beginning!" groaned Betty Lou. "We'll never get to V for Vanilla. . . ."

"Let me see now. I will try to continue," said Grover. "We are up to the letter M for Mushroom Mango Mash—*my* special favorite. For N we have Nifty Noodle Nectar. O is for Orange Oyster Oops!, P—Pickle Parfait, Q—Quacky Quip. (Is that not a ducky flavor?) R—Ravioli Ripple."

The stack of scoops got higher and higher. Herbie's and Betty Lou's eyes got bigger and bigger as they watched the leaning tower of scoops.

"Oh, my gosh. It's going to fall!" said Betty Lou.

"Do not worry. I, Grover, will not let these scoops fall down." He swayed back and forth, barely balancing the tipsy tower of ice cream.

"Hey, Betty Lou," whispered Herbie. "This is better than the circus."

"Phew," said Grover, as he steadied the scoops. "That was a very close call. Thank goodness I was tops in balancing at Scoop School. Now, Herbie, do you see anything here that you like? I do not want to rush you, but this cone is getting very difficult to balance—even for Grover."

"I haven't seen all the flavors yet," said Herbie.

"Oh, that is right," said Grover. "I nearly forgot. Now, what letter was I up to?"

"You were up to S, mister," said Betty Lou.

"S!" said Grover. "Scrumptious S for Sardine Swirl." Then he dipped into the ice-cream bin marked T—for Triple Turkey Trifle. "And now we have U—for Upside-down Uglifruit. . . . And now, V—V for Vanilla. . . ."

"That's it! That's the one!" cried Betty Lou, jumping up and down

with joy. "I'll have a Vanilla cone, please."

"Oh! Oh! I am so sorry, little girl," said Grover. "But I cannot stop until I get to the end of the alphabet."

Grover dashed over to the bin marked W. He quickly scooped out Watermelon Wobble.

"Now on to the X flavor... XXXXXXX.That stands for many kisses. (You would *love* this flavor!) It is even better than Y for Yak Yogurt Yum-Yum.

"Oh, my goodness," said Grover. "Only one more flavor to go. I think I can do it." Grover dipped his furry little arm into the last bin at the far, far end of the counter. He brought out the Z scoop—Zucchini Zip. The twenty-sixth and last scoop!

"Oh! Oh! I am so-o-o-o-o pooped," wheezed poor Grover as he staggered around under the dripping tower of scoops. "They never told me it would be like this back in Scoop School. Herbie, please—tell me which flavor you want. One scoop or two? Plain or with sprinkles?"

"Well...ummmm...errrr... geeee..." said Herbie.

"Herbie! Make up your mind," wailed Betty Lou. "You've seen every flavor in the place, and I want my Vanilla!"

Herbie thought about it and thought about it. He thought for a *long* time. Finally, he looked up at Grover and said, "Wellll... ummmm...maybe if you started all over from the beginning..."

"WHAT?" shrieked Grover. "All over again from the beginning!!!"

Grover threw up his hands, launching the enormous cone straight up in the air. Ice cream flew in all directions.

"He's going bananas!" said Betty Lou.

"Gee, mister," said Herbie. "Don't get so upset. I'll take Vanilla, too!"

"EEEEEEEYYYYYYYYIIIIIII!" screamed Grover, and he fainted away right into the AnchovyApplesauce–BaloneyBonbon–CactusCrunch–DinosaurDip–EggplantEclair–FruitcakeFiestaFlip–GumballGoop–HoneyHamburger Hash–ImitationIgloo–JiffyJellybeanJive–KangarooKringle–LavenderLicorice–MushroomMangoMash–NiftyNoodleNectar–OrangeOysterOops!–PickleParfait–QuackyQuip–RavioliRipple–SardineSwirl–TripleTurkeyTrifle–Upside-downUglifruit–Vanilla–WatermelonWobble–XXXXXXX–YakYogurtYumYum–ZucchiniZip!

Can you find 15 Twiddlebugs?

Mary had a little lamb.
Its fleece was white as snow.
And everywhere that Mary went,
The lamb was
sure to go.

Which Yo-yo?

Ernie wants to give Bert a yo-yo that is not like the others.
Which one is different?

1, 2 Green and Blue!

What numbers are green?
What numbers are blue?
What numbers are yellow?
What numbers are brown?
What numbers are orange?
What numbers are black?
What numbers are red?

6

2

11

13

1

15

10

3

8

7